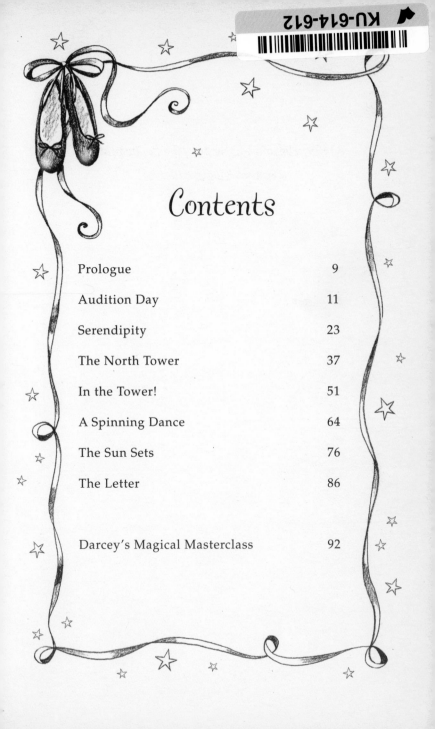

Contents

Prologue   9

Audition Day   11

Serendipity   23

The North Tower   37

In the Tower!   51

A Spinning Dance   64

The Sun Sets   76

The Letter   86

Darcey's Magical Masterclass   92

Magic Ballerina
Rosa and the Magic Dream

Welcome to the world of Enchantia!

I have always loved to dance. The captivating
music and wonderful stories of ballet are so
inspiring. So come with me and let's follow
Rosa on her magical adventures in
Enchantia, where the stories of dance will
take you on a very special journey...

[signature]

p.s. Turn to the back to learn a special
dance step from me...

Special thanks to
Linda Chapman and
Nellie Ryan

First published in Great Britain by HarperCollins Children's Books 2009
HarperCollins Children's Books is a division of HarperCollins Publishers Ltd,
77-85 Fulham Palace Road, Hammersmith, London W6 8JB

The HarperCollins website address is
www.harpercollins.co.uk

1

Text copyright © HarperCollins Children's Books 2009
Illustrations by Nellie Ryan
Illustrations copyright © HarperCollins Children's Books 2009

MAGIC BALLERINA™ and the 'Magic Ballerina' logo are
trademarks of HarperCollins Publishers Ltd.

ISBN 978 0 00 785919 1

Printed and bound in England by
Clays Ltd, St Ives plc

Magic Ballerina ™

Rosa and the Magic Dream

Darcey Bussell

HarperCollins *Children's Books*

To Phoebe and Zoe, as they are the inspiration behind Magic Ballerina.

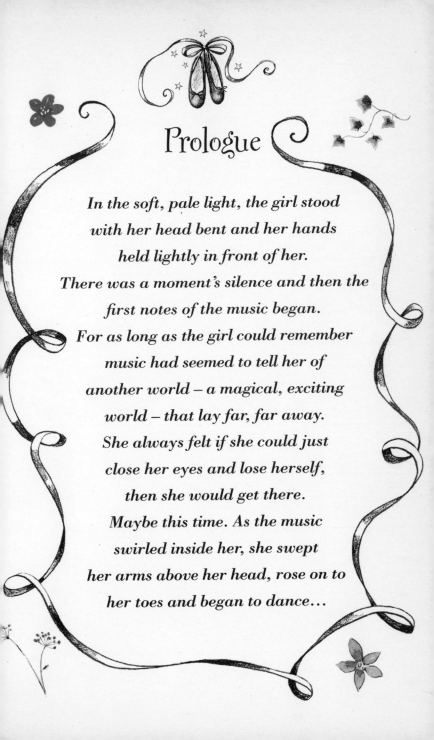

Prologue

In the soft, pale light, the girl stood
with her head bent and her hands
held lightly in front of her.
There was a moment's silence and then the
first notes of the music began.
For as long as the girl could remember
music had seemed to tell her of
another world – a magical, exciting
world – that lay far, far away.
She always felt if she could just
close her eyes and lose herself,
then she would get there.
Maybe this time. As the music
swirled inside her, she swept
her arms above her head, rose on to
her toes and began to dance…

Audition Day

Rosa Maitland stood nervously in the queue of parents and girls waiting to go into the large ballet studio. Her best friend, Olivia, was beside her, chewing her lip. *I can't believe we're here and we're actually about to audition for the Royal Ballet School!* Rosa thought.

It still seemed like some impossible dream. Could it really be just a few months back that Rosa and Olivia, and some of the other girls who went to Madame Za-Za's dance school, had been invited to audition for White Lodge, the junior part of the Royal Ballet School?

It was a boarding school, and as well as doing normal lessons, the students had dancing classes every day. It was very hard to get in, and although Rosa and three of the other girls from school had made it through the Preliminary Auditions, the Final Auditions would be much harder. Rosa's stomach felt like it was full of butterflies as they walked into the studio. "I feel so nervous."

"Me too," muttered Olivia.

Rosa spotted Delphie and Sukie, the other girls from Madame Za-Za's ballet school.

Rosa really liked Delphie, but she didn't usually get on with Sukie, who could be a bit mean. Delphie waved. Olivia and Rosa headed over to where they were sitting.

"Hi," Rosa said as their parents all greeted each other.

Sukie just nodded coolly, but Delphie looked delighted to see them. "Hi." She glanced round. "There are loads of people auditioning, aren't there?"

Rosa nodded. There were around forty girls in the studio, but only about twelve girls would get picked. *And everyone here will be really good*, Rosa reminded herself as she sat down.

A lady in a black top walked to the front. Imogen Green, Rosa thought, recognising the Head of Auditions. Imogen clapped her hands and silence fell.

"Welcome to White Lodge, everyone," Imogen said, smiling at them. "It's lovely to see you all. I'll start by explaining how the day will be run."

Imogen told the girls that they would be split into two groups,

14

each of which would take part in a dance class, do some writing, be seen by a doctor to check they were healthy, have an interview with the headteacher and go on a tour of the school. It all sounded very exciting!

When Imogen finished talking, the girls were split up. Delphie and Sukie were in one group and Olivia and Rosa in another – their group was dancing first.

"Phew!" Rosa whispered to Olivia as they got changed and helped each other with their hair. Finally Rosa took her red ballet shoes out of her bag and slipped them on. As she did up the ribbons, she smiled to herself.

After all, her shoes were very special. Sometimes, with no warning, they would start to sparkle and whisk her away to the magical land of Enchantia, where the characters from all the different ballets lived. Rosa thought about some of the amazing adventures she'd had there and the people she had met…

"Rosa, come on!" Olivia said, nudging her.

Looking up, Rosa saw that the other girls were lining up at the door. She tucked in the ends of the ribbons and jumped to her feet.

"Good luck!" she said to her friend as they joined the others.

Olivia forced a nervous smile. "You too."

As soon as the dance class started, Rosa felt

her nerves disappear. She concentrated on
the familiar exercises, her whole mind
focusing on bending and stretching, thinking
about the line of her arms, pointing her toes
and lengthening her back. She enjoyed
herself so much she almost forgot that there
were six examiners watching her!

After the dance class, the girls met up with their parents for juice and biscuits, then went off with the rest of their group to a classroom where they had to write about what they wanted to be and what they liked doing. Rosa wrote as much as she could about her life and her dreams of becoming a ballerina.

Finally, after seeing the doctor, it was time for their interviews with the headteacher. When Olivia went in, Rosa waited outside the room.

Sukie came along the corridor. "Hi, Rosa," she said. "Are you waiting for your turn?"

Rosa nodded.

"I've done mine," Sukie told her. "Have you seen the dorms where the girls sleep yet?"

"No." Rosa had been longing to look around the school, but she had been kept so busy she hadn't had a chance.

"They're cool!" said Sukie. "And they're just up these stairs. Come on, why don't we go now before your interview? I'll show you where they are."

Rosa felt tempted but shook her head. "I'd better not. It'll be my turn in a minute. Olivia's in there now."

"She'll be ages," said Sukie. "You've easily got time to run upstairs with me and have a look. Come on!"

Rosa hesitated. "Um…"

19

"We'll be really quick," Sukie said persuasively.

"Oh, all right!" Rosa jumped to her feet. *No, don't*, a little voice in her head said. But she ignored it. *It'll be fine*, she told herself.

"It's this way!" Sukie raced away up the staircase.

Picking up her bag, Rosa followed her…

The stairs curved round. At the top there was a small landing and three corridors leading in different directions. Sukie had vanished. Rosa looked around. Where was she?

"Sukie!" she called.

But there was no reply.

A horrible thought crossed Rosa's mind.

Was Sukie playing a trick on her? Maybe she wanted Rosa to get lost and be late for her interview? But surely not even Sukie would be that mean? Rosa hesitated, unsure what to do.

A tinkle of sweet music echoed through the air and at that very same moment she felt a tingling against her shoulder where she was holding her bag.

She caught her breath. Did her ballet shoes really want to take her to Enchantia right now?

She hesitated for a moment, then unzipped her bag. Sure enough, inside it, her red shoes were glowing and sparkling.

21

She stopped herself, uncertain whether to put them on or not. It wasn't exactly the best timing. But then again, Rosa knew that the shoes only took her to Enchantia when the characters really needed her help. *It's OK*, she quickly reminded herself, *no time will pass here while I'm gone.* Heart thumping, Rosa quickly pulled on her shoes. A glittering mist of colour surrounded her and she felt herself being twirled around and magically swept away…

Serendipity

The magic set Rosa down in a strangely familiar forest. There were frosty trees all around and birds singing in the leafless branches. For a moment, Rosa wondered if it was the same place she had been when she had rescued the magical Firebird. She shuddered as she thought of the horrible Wicked Fairy who had imprisoned him.

"Hello?" Rosa called hesitantly.
"Nutmeg? Nutmeg, are you here?"

Nutmeg was the Fairy of the Spices. The
fairy usually met Rosa when she arrived in
Enchantia. But today there was no sign of her.

Spotting a path through the trees, Rosa
headed down it. As she reached the main
track, she heard a faint noise through the
trees behind her – like someone crying out.
She spun round. What was it?

"Hello?" she called again.
But there was no answer.

Then, suddenly, a carriage pulled by two white horses with silver plumes and golden bridles came around the bend in the track ahead of her. The driver was dressed in white breeches and a coat embroidered with gold thread. Rosa expected the carriage to sweep straight past but, to her surprise, it stopped. The driver jumped down and opened the carriage door.

Rosa stared as she saw a beautiful lady
with long blonde
hair and a pink
sparkly dress
sitting inside.

"Hello," said
the lady. "You
must be Rosa."

"Yes, yes I am," Rosa
replied, feeling almost like she should
curtsy. Who was this beautiful lady?

The lady smiled. "I thought you must
be. My name's Serendipity. I'm a friend
of Nutmeg's."

Rosa noticed the wings on her back. "So,
you're a fairy too," she said.

"Yes," the lady laughed gently. "I'm so

glad I found you. Nutmeg can't come to meet you so she sent me instead. Get into my carriage and we'll go to my castle."

Rosa hesitated. She wasn't sure whether she should get into a strange carriage, even when the owner of it was a friend of Nutmeg's.

"Oh, do get in," Serendipity urged. "It's so cold out. When we get back I'll get us some hot chocolate and biscuits. Nutmeg will join us there."

The air was frosty and after such a long day at the auditions, Rosa was feeling hungry and thirsty. She got into the carriage and the driver shut the door with a bang.

As he did so, Rosa was sure she heard a faint cry of "Rosa!"

She looked round. "What was that?"

"I didn't hear anything," said Serendipity, shrugging.

"Someone said my name!"

"Drive on!" Serendipity called to the driver.

"But…"

However, it was too late – the driver had brought the reins down on the horses' backs. They plunged forward, pulling the carriage down the track. Rosa felt a prickling sense of unease, but she put it to the back of her mind.

The woods flashed by outside the carriage.

"Look, there's my castle!" Serendipity said as the horses cantered out of the trees.

Rosa saw a beautiful castle with pointed turrets lying just ahead of them. It was just like something from a fairytale!

"Wow!" breathed Rosa. "It's amazing!"

The carriage swept through the gates and down the driveway. Three servants hurried out as the carriage stopped.

"This way," said Serendipity as she stepped out of the carriage. "Let's go in."

Rosa jumped out and followed the fairy into a grand entrance hall that had a sweeping staircase. There were rich rugs hanging on the walls and a fire burning in a large grate. There were ornaments on tables and little lamps. It felt very cosy and Rosa breathed a sigh of relief as she felt the warmth seep into her cold bones. What had she been so anxious about?

"We'll have hot chocolate and cakes in the lilac drawing room, Lizadora," Serendipity said to a maid who bobbed a quick curtsy and hurried off.

Rosa looked around the hall; it was wide

and spacious with a polished wood floor
and she couldn't resist dancing forward a
few paces and spinning round...

"Stop!" Serendipity spoke sharply.

Rosa came to a standstill and looked at
her in astonishment.

"I mean, watch you don't knock one of
the ornaments over," Serendipity corrected
herself, giving Rosa a reassuring look.

"Sorry, I know that sounds silly, but
I wouldn't want you to hurt yourself."

She took her silver slippers off and
placed them by the door. "Now, why don't
you take your shoes off and come into the
drawing room with me?"

"Take my shoes off?" Rosa echoed.

Serendipity nodded. "There's no need to

wear shoes in the drawing room – we don't
want to get mud on the carpets now, do we?"

Rosa looked down at her ballet shoes. She
didn't want to take them off,
but what could she do?
Refusing to would be really
rude to Nutmeg's friend.
Reluctantly she untied the
ribbons and stepped out of
her shoes.

One of the servants
immediately came over
and picked them up.
"What are you doing?" Rosa asked in
alarm.

"Don't worry. He'll take your shoes up
to your bedroom," said Serendipity.

"I could keep them with me," Rosa suggested. But the servant had already carried them away and Serendipity didn't seem to have heard. She was already heading through one of the doors. Rosa swallowed, but decided to be polite and not make a fuss as she stepped into the drawing room.

Inside, the carpet was a spotless cream and the curtains, a delicate shade of lilac. Garlands of purple and white flowers were strung around the walls. On a small table with chairs were two steaming mugs of hot chocolate on a silver tray.

Serendipity handed Rosa a mug.

Rosa sat down and sipped the delicious warm drink. It tasted like real melted

chocolate. After only a few sips, she
yawned. It had been such a busy day and
now waves of tiredness were sweeping
over Rosa. Her head felt strangely
muddled. She was sure there was
something or someone she should be
asking about, but she couldn't quite
remember who.

"You look very sleepy," Serendipity said
softly. "Why don't you have a nap after
you've had something to eat?"

Rosa smiled at the fairy's sweet face. She
looked so kind and caring...

"Here's the food now," Serendipity said as
the maid came back in with a tray of toasted
teacakes and buttered crumpets. Rosa's
tummy rumbled and she took a teacake. But

as she bit into it and tasted the spicy warmth, an image of a fairy in a pale pink and brown tutu popped into her head. *Nutmeg!*

"Is Nutmeg here?" she asked, sitting up in her chair.

"Not yet," Serendipity said. "Don't worry, she will be soon, though. Now, why don't you try one of these instead?" She whisked the teacake out of Rosa's hands and gave her a crumpet.

Rosa looked at her in surprise, but did as she was told and tried the other pastry. As she bit into it, thoughts of Nutmeg faded away and tiredness swept over her. She could hardly keep her eyes open. She'd just close them for a few moments. Her eyelids fluttered and the next moment she had fallen fast asleep…

The North Tower

Rosa woke up in a soft, springy bed, feeling confused. Where was she? *Of course!* she remembered. *I'm in Serendipity's castle. I must have fallen asleep in the drawing room.* She could remember drinking the hot chocolate, eating the crumpet, shutting her eyes…

Pushing the covers back, Rosa got out of bed and went to the window. The sun was just rising. She must have been asleep a whole night!

Her clothes had been laid out neatly on a chair. On the floor beside the chair was a pair of pretty golden slippers embroidered with sparkling thread. Rosa got dressed and started to put the slippers on, but as she did so, she paused. Something didn't feel right.

She looked at the shoes and remembered Serendipity saying the servant would put her shoes in her bedroom. *These must be my shoes*, she thought. After all, they're here with

38

my clothes. So why did they feel wrong?

Red shoes... The thought buzzed around Rosa's head for a moment, but then faded away.

Shrugging, Rosa put on the golden slippers and went to the door. It led out on to a corridor and down a grand staircase. A door opened at the bottom and Serendipity came out.

"Rosa! You're up!" she said, smiling.

"Thank you for letting me stay." Rosa rubbed her head. "Serendipity, are you sure these are *my* shoes?"

"Of course they are!" Serendipity laughed gaily. "Now, come on, let's go and have some breakfast. It's so lovely having a guest. You will stay for a while, won't you?"

Rosa nodded and scratched her head. "Of course!"

Breakfast was delicious – pancakes and fresh fruit – and afterwards, Serendipity showed Rosa around the gardens. Then they came back inside and sat reading and playing cards. It was very pleasant, but Rosa had a strange nagging feeling that there was something she should be doing, she just couldn't remember what.

At teatime, the maid came in with some teacakes. Serendipity quickly shook her head. "No teacakes today. Could you fetch us some iced buns instead, Lizadora?"

As the maid turned to leave the room, the

sweet, spicy scent of the teacakes wafted over to Rosa and a word popped into her head. "Nutmeg," she said suddenly.

"Yes, you're right, there's nutmeg in the teacakes," said Serendipity quickly. "And I don't like nutmeg."

Rosa frowned. She was sure she hadn't meant there was nutmeg in the teacakes, but she wasn't actually sure why the word had come into her head like that. She felt like there was someone she should be seeing or something she should be doing. It was all too confusing! She sank back into her chair and rested her cheek on her hand.

The next morning passed in a similar way. After lunch, Rosa had a nap. When she got up, she wandered downstairs. Lizadora was moving between rooms. "Is Serendipity here?" Rosa asked.

The maid's dark eyes stared at the ground. "She's gone out. You can do whatever you want, she said, but you're not to go into the North Tower."

"The North Tower? Why not?"

"I-I don't know," the maid stuttered. "She just said." And that seemed to be that.

Rosa hesitated, but then she started to explore the castle. There were lots of rooms and corridors. After a little while she came

to some stairs labelled NORTH TOWER.
I shouldn't go there, she remembered.

She was about to turn away when a thought flickered across her mind.

Why not?

She looked at the staircase. She felt heavy and slow, but deep inside there was a spark of curiosity burning. It grew stronger. Why shouldn't she go there? She could just go and have a quick look…

And so she went up the stairs. They twisted round and round and at the top, she found a small blue door. Rosa turned the brass handle and found that it led into a circular room.

Going inside, she stopped and stared. In a glass case on the other side of the room there was a pair of beautiful red shoes with ribbons…

Ballet shoes!

Deep in her mind, Rosa felt a memory stir.

She was sure she'd seen these shoes before. She didn't know why, but for some reason she knew that they were important.

Going over, she opened the glass case. As she touched the soft leather, her fingers tingled. A single thought suddenly filled her mind. She had to put them on! Impulsively she pulled them out of the case. As she tied the ribbons, the tiredness that had been weighing her down fell away. Suddenly she wanted to run and jump and dance…

DANCE! The thought banged into her brain. She'd forgotten all about dancing! She spun round and then jumped in the air, her feet crossing over. She landed in second position and skipped around the room, before stopping on her toes, arms above her head. In that moment, the haze in her mind cleared and everything came flooding back.

The shoes were her magic ballet shoes! *They were taken from me,* she remembered.

*Serendipity must have told the servants to
put them up here so I wouldn't find them.
And what about Nutmeg? I was supposed
to be meeting her here.*

An icy hand seemed to grasp at Rosa's
heart. Serendipity must have put a spell on
her to make her forget everything…

Rosa ran down the winding staircase,
suddenly becoming aware of shouting and
raised voices. A manservant was running
along the landing at the bottom of the
staircase, but he didn't look normal. He
seemed to be shimmering, dissolving and a
long green tail was growing… Rosa gasped
out loud as, in front of her very eyes, the
servant turned into a big green lizard!

She'd barely had time to take it in before

she realised that all around her, the walls of the castle were shimmering and dissolving too. White carpets turned to black stone, tapestries disappeared from the walls, soft lights were being replaced by dark candles in spiky metal holders. What was happening?

The castle and the servants must have all

been enchanted, Rosa realised. *And now the spell has somehow broken and they're turning back to how they were!*

She didn't know what was going on, but she definitely wanted to get out of there. Racing for the front door, Rosa threw it open and ran outside. But as she did so, she saw Serendipity's carriage charging

down the drive. The horses were turning into two giant mice and the coachman was becoming a lizard, just like the servants in the house. The carriage's gleaming white sides were darkening to black. It skidded to a stop in front of the house and the door swung open.

"No!" Rosa whispered in horror as a grey-haired woman in a dark, ragged dress and a long beaky nose stepped out. It was the Wicked Fairy of Enchantia!

In the Tower!

The Wicked Fairy laughed gloatingly. She was just as ugly and horrid as Rosa remembered her. "How do you like my castle now, Rosa?" she demanded.

"*Your* castle?" Rosa stammered. "So you're Serendipity?"

The Wicked Fairy grinned. "Indeed! I cast a magical disguise over myself and the castle, and enchanted you to make you forget everything."

"But why?" Rosa asked helplessly.

"I wanted to stop you from going to the Ruling Ceremony, that's why," the Wicked Fairy cackled.

"The Ruling Ceremony?" Rosa echoed. "What's that?"

"Don't you know anything, you stupid girl?" snapped the fairy. "The King and Queen have special magic protecting them so that no one can 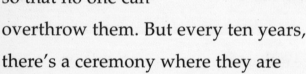 overthrow them. But every ten years, there's a ceremony where they are reappointed as the rulers of Enchantia by the First Fairy…"

Rosa knew the First Fairy. She was very magical and had been there when Enchantia had been created.

"To summon her, the human who is the guardian of the red ballet shoes must dance in the centre of the forest, just as the sun sets," the Wicked Fairy went on. "The ballet shoes can bring her here because they are part of the ancient magic of Enchantia." She cackled. "But this year, the First Fairy will not be summoned because you and the ballet shoes will not be there!"

"So, what will happen?" Rosa asked in alarm.

The Wicked Fairy drew herself up. "The

magic spells protecting the King and
Queen will vanish as the sun sets and I
will then be able to use my magic against
them. I shall become queen!"

"No," Rosa whispered.

"Oh, yes," the Fairy gloated. "And it's
all your fault, Rosa. If you'd waited and
met Nutmeg in the woods like you should
have done, you would have been safely
whisked off to the Royal Palace to have
your role in the ceremony explained by the
King and Queen. Instead you came with
me and now…" She banged her wand on
the ground. A mist appeared and in the
centre of it Rosa saw a picture. It showed
Queen Isabella crying and King Tristan
comforting her and everyone else in the

Royal Palace running around frantically.
"Where's Rosa?" Rosa heard them saying.
"Where's Nutmeg? We need them!"

"What do they mean, where's Nutmeg?"
Rosa demanded.

The Wicked Fairy chuckled. "I'm afraid
Nutmeg had a little accident while she was
on her way to meet you."

"What sort of accident?" Rosa asked.

"That doesn't matter. What matters is that she can't get to you and you're stuck here. No one is going to find you and you won't be going to the ceremony!"

Rosa made a dash past the Wicked Fairy.

"Guards, get her!" the hag snapped.

Four lizards followed Rosa out of the house and caught her in seconds.

"Let me go!" she protested, struggling as they gripped her arms.

"Certainly not!" replied the Wicked Fairy.

Rosa kept struggling. "I don't understand. Why did you do the enchantment? Why did you bother to disguise yourself and your castle? Why not just stop me with magic?"

"Because just as there are spells
protecting the King and Queen, there are
spells that protect the ceremony. No one
can use magic to stop the guardian of the
ballet shoes going to the ceremony. You
had to come with me willingly – and you
did. You believed I was a beautiful, kind
fairy. Now, you have broken my
enchantment by dancing in my castle with

those shoes, but that does not matter.
The ceremony will happen this evening –
but you shall not be there. Guards!"
She looked at the lizards. "Throw her
in the tower until it is over."

"No!" cried Rosa. But the
guards were already
pulling her towards a
door at the base of
a tower. Rosa
was pushed
inside and the
heavy door
banged shut
behind her.
She heard great
bolts being shot across.

She flung herself at the thick wood and beat on it with her fists. "Let me out!" she cried furiously.

"No!" cackled the Wicked Fairy from the other side. Rosa heard her stomp away and the main door to the castle slam shut.

Slowly she looked all around. It was dark inside the tower, with only a little light filtering through one small window high up near the top of the tower. The walls and floor were completely bare.

59

Rosa sank down to the floor, tears welling in her eyes. She'd been so stupid! Why had she got into the carriage? *The Wicked Fairy was right*, thought Rosa. *It is all my fault!* She didn't usually cry, but now a sob burst from her.

A silvery voice rang out. "Oh, dearie me. You don't seem very happy, poppet."

Rosa almost jumped out of her skin. Rubbing her tears away with her hands, she looked around the dark dungeon, but it was completely empty. "Where... where are you?" she stammered.

"I'm over here, dearie."

The voice came from Rosa's left. She looked but there was just the wall of the dungeon.

She stepped closer to the wall, her eyes
scanning through the shadows, when
suddenly she saw a spider, sitting in the
middle of a web. Rosa squealed and
jumped back.

"Don't be scared." The spider smiled
and waved a hairy leg. "I'm Tangleweb.
Hello, dearie."

Rosa backed away
across the dungeon.
"H-hello," she
quavered. She didn't
really like spiders all that much.

"Oh, it's so lovely to see someone else,"
said Tangleweb. "I've been shut in here
on my own for ages, feeling very lonely.
Why have you been put in here, my dear?"

Rosa explained what had happened. As she told the story she found herself stepping closer to Tangleweb again. The spider might look scary, but she seemed quite friendly. She had started to spin her web as Rosa talked and her spinning movements reminded Rosa of dancing.

"Goodness me!" Tangleweb exclaimed, as Rosa finished her story. "This is dreadful news. We really must get you out of here, poppet!"

Rosa glanced round. "But how?"

Tangleweb spun her web for a moment, deep in thought. "Hmm… she has the shoes," she said, almost to herself. "She can obviously dance." She stopped and looked at Rosa. "Can you climb a rope, dearie?"

Rosa nodded.

The spider smiled. "Then, maybe I can help…"

A Spinning Dance

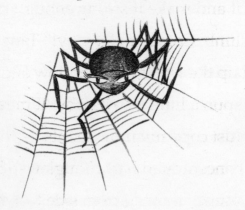

Tangleweb looked at Rosa. "I'll go up to the window and spin a thread down for you to climb up."

Rosa's heart sank. "But I'm much too heavy!"

"Ah, but we will use the shoes' magic, dearie," said Tangleweb. "If you dance a spinning dance as I spin my thread, and if you copy my movements exactly, the magic in your shoes will strengthen the thread, thicken it and make it strong enough for you to climb. Come on, let's try!" Tangleweb scuttled up the wall to the window and quickly spun a little web nearby. "I'm ready to start. Just copy my movements."

Rosa concentrated hard. Tangleweb began to twirl round, moving from side to side, and Rosa followed her. Step to the left and back. Step to the right and back. Spin round. Do it again. She moved around the dungeon floor, copying the spider as Tangleweb began to spin a long strand of silver thread. Sparks swirled up from Rosa's shoes. She gasped and almost stopped.

"Keep going!" Tangleweb urged.

The sparks wound round the
thread, flashing in the
darkness. Rosa kept
dancing and Tangleweb
kept spinning, until the
thread got thicker and
a silky rope of
it hung down
from the
window.

"There!"
cried Tangleweb
triumphantly.

Rosa stopped
dancing. "I can
reach it!" she cried.

The sparkles vanished

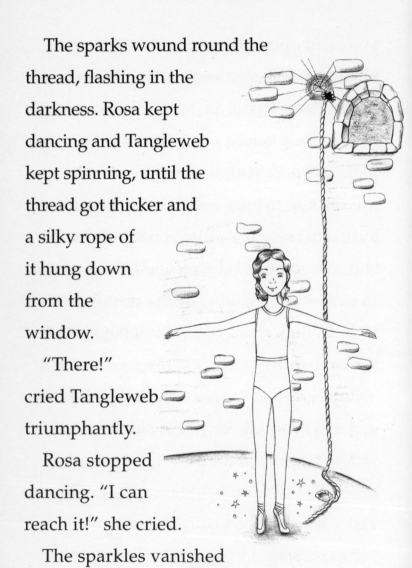

as Rosa stopped dancing, but the rope remained. "Then come on, dearie, up you come. There's no time to lose!" Tangleweb called. She glanced out of the window. "The sun is starting to set."

Gripping the rope with her knees, Rosa pulled herself upwards, hand over hand. She went on until she reached the top. Tangleweb was sitting in the middle of her web, smiling. "Oh, well done, poppet!" she exclaimed.

Rosa grasped the window ledge. It was just wide enough for her to climb on to. From there she could see out over the castle grounds and all the way to the forest. The Wicked Fairy's words rang in her head: *The magic spells protecting the King and Queen will vanish as the sun sets and I will then be able to use my magic against them.* Rosa knew she had to get there now!

To her relief, the window wasn't locked. Rosa pulled it open, hauled up the rope and hung it down the outside of the tower. She looked round at the little spider. "Thank you for helping me, Tangleweb. What are you going to do now?"

"Come with you, dearie, of course!" said the spider. "I'd have escaped long ago if I could have opened this window. Maybe I could travel with you?"

Rosa nodded. "Of course." Her fear of

the spider had completely vanished. She picked up Tangleweb, who felt warm and tickly, popped the creature on her shoulder and started climbing down the rope. She didn't know what she would do if anybody saw her, but she had to risk it.

Reaching the bottom of the tower, Rosa let go of the rope and ran as fast as she could across the grass. She reached the safety of the trees, panting and gasping, and dragged in huge gulps of air.

Tangleweb coughed. "Oh, dearie, I don't like to say this, but there's really no time to stop and rest."

Rosa knew Tangleweb was right. The sun was setting in the sky. She broke into a run again. They had to get to the centre of the forest – before it was too late!

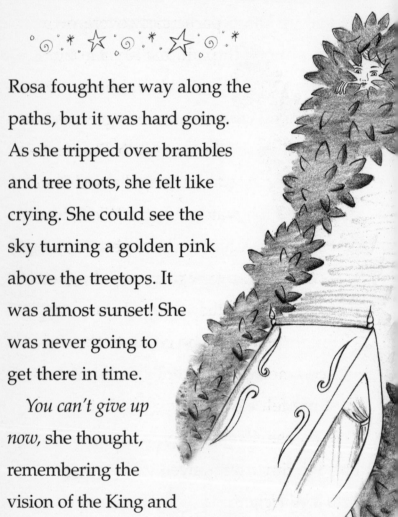

Rosa fought her way along the
paths, but it was hard going.
As she tripped over brambles
and tree roots, she felt like
crying. She could see the
sky turning a golden pink
above the treetops. It
was almost sunset! She
was never going to
get there in time.

*You can't give up
now,* she thought,
remembering the
vision of the King and

Queen as she pushed her way along a particularly overgrown path. *You've got to try.*

Suddenly she heard the creak of carriage wheels on the main path. She ducked down behind a bush and watched as the Wicked Fairy raced past in her black carriage, the driver whipping the giant mice as they charged along.

"She must be going to the ceremony!" the spider exclaimed.

Rosa felt a sob rise up inside her. "It's no use. We're not going to get there in time, Tangleweb."

"Help! Help!"

Rosa blinked. "That sounds like… Nutmeg!"

The voice had come from just ahead of them. Rosa broke into a run.

"Oh, my goodness!" she gasped as she saw what lay ahead of her. Nutmeg was trapped inside a giant wooden birdcage that was lying on its side in the bottom of a ditch. She looked very dishevelled and her wand was lying on the ground.

"Rosa!" she cried, her face lighting up.
"It's you!"

"What happened?" Rosa said as the
spider waved at the fairy.

"Oh, Rosa," Nutmeg cried unhappily.
"I was supposed to meet you and take
you to the palace. I was waiting for you
when the Wicked Fairy's lizards grabbed
me. They locked me in this cage, rolled it
over and pushed it into the ditch. I dropped
my wand so I couldn't magic myself away. I
thought I heard your voice and I called out to
you, but you didn't come."

Rosa felt dreadful. "I met the Wicked Fairy,
only she was in disguise, so I went with her
to her castle and she enchanted me," she said,
shamefaced. "I got away, but I'm not going

to get to the centre of the forest by the time the sun sets. Oh, Nutmeg, what can we do?"

"It's not quite sunset yet," said Nutmeg. "If you can get me out of this cage, I can whisk us to the centre of the forest with my magic."

Rosa ran to the cage. "Oh. There's no key in the lock," she said.

"Then it really is too late," said Nutmeg in a small voice.

"No, it isn't!" cried Tangleweb. "Let me help, dearies." She scuttled over and jumped on to the cage. The next moment the little spider had disappeared inside the lock! "If I can fiddle about inside…" There were a few mutterings and a couple of clicks and then the cage door sprang open. Tangleweb poked her head out. "Easy!"

"Oh, Tangleweb. You're brilliant!"
gasped Rosa. She scooped the spider up.
"Thank you!"

Nutmeg climbed out of the cage and
picked up her wand. She waved it in the
air and grabbed Rosa's hands. "Hang on,
Tangleweb!" she called. "Here we go!"

The Sun Sets

Rosa, Nutmeg and Tangleweb were
whisked through the air and set gently
down in the trees at the edge of a glade,
where King Tristan and Queen Isabella
were sitting on golden thrones. All around
them were people Rosa knew, but her
eyes focused on the Wicked Fairy, who
was standing in the centre of the clearing,

her back to Rosa and Nutmeg, cackling with glee.

"Your time is up!" she said, pointing her bony finger at the King and Queen. "The girl and the shoes are not here. Prepare to rule Enchantia no more!"

Nutmeg pushed Rosa. "Rosa, Rosa… dance!" she hissed.

"What type of dance?" Rosa whispered back.

"Anything! It's just important that you dance."

Rosa didn't stop to question. Sweeping her arms around her head, she ran forward with flowing steps before stopping on her toes and reaching up to the sky. Then she skipped in a circle before turning round.

The people near the edge of the clearing saw her and gasped. But the Wicked Fairy was too busy advancing on the King and Queen to notice. "It is *my* turn to rule now!" she screeched.

"We'll see about that," Rosa cried, turning round and raising one knee.

The Wicked Fairy swung about. "You!" She raised her wand, but she was too late. Rosa was so well rehearsed that nothing could distract her.

Beautiful music flooded out through the air and golden sparkles started to swirl around the trees like dancing fireflies. Everyone gasped as there was a bright flash and a fairy appeared, spinning round on her pointes in the clearing. The First Fairy!

Rosa sank into a deep curtsy. All around her, everyone else either curtsied or bowed too...

Everyone except the Wicked Fairy. "No!" she shrieked, running towards the First Fairy, who pointed her wand straight at her.

The Wicked Fairy suddenly fell over.

She tried to stand up again but the First
Fairy had obviously put a charm on her
legs. Every time the Wicked Fairy tried to
stand, she fell over again.

"What have you done!" she shouted.
"Take this magic off me! Take it off and—"
The First Fairy pointed her wand at the
Wicked Fairy's mouth and the Wicked
Fairy's voice stopped. Looking startled, the
Wicked Fairy opened and closed her mouth

like a goldfish. Rosa grinned. It was very funny seeing the Wicked Fairy looking so silly! Around the clearing, the watchers nudged each other and pointed.

The First Fairy looked at her and spoke in a sweet but grave voice. "Wicked Fairy, you tried to stop the Ruling Ceremony. That is against the rules of Enchantia. For that you must be punished. You will be banished to the furthest reaches of the land. In a year's time, you may return to the Royal Palace, and if you are truly sorry, you may beg a pardon from the King and Queen. Then you will be allowed to return to your castle. Until then, be gone and learn the error of your ways!"

The Wicked Fairy started to shake her

fists, but the First Fairy waved her wand and the next second, the Wicked Fairy had disappeared. Everyone burst out clapping and cheering.

The First Fairy danced over to the King and Queen. "I give you magic to rule Enchantia for another ten years, King Tristan and Queen Isabella," she said, her voice ringing out. "May they be happy and peaceful ones for us all." She touched the King and Queen with her wand and then the music started to play again. Moving in perfect time, the fairy danced lightly around the thrones before spinning off around the clearing.

As she came to where Nutmeg and Rosa were standing, her eyes met Rosa's and she smiled. Rosa smiled back in delight. The fairy ran to the centre and leaped upwards in a *grand jeté*, one leg forward, one back, her arms stretched out to the sides. Then, at the height of the jump, she suddenly vanished. The music stopped and a shower of sparkles fell through the air.

For a moment there was silence and then everyone started talking at once. The King and Queen ran over to Rosa and Nutmeg.

Nutmeg swung Rosa round. "You did it! You saved the day!"

"Only with help from you and Tangleweb," said Rosa. She stopped spinning for a moment and reached for the spider.

Tangleweb smiled happily. "It looks as if it all worked out perfectly!"

"So what are you going to do now, Tangleweb?" asked Rosa.

Nutmeg looked shyly at the spider. "You can come and live with me, if you'd like."

"Sounds lovely, dearie," Tangleweb nodded at Nutmeg. "So much better than being stuck in that horrible dungeon for ever more."

Rosa couldn't help herself from laughing when, at that moment, she felt her feet starting to tingle. "Oh, wow! I'm about to go!" she called out, realising that her shoes were glowing as her work here was done. "Bye, Nutmeg. Bye, Tangleweb. Bye, everyone!"

"Bye, Rosa!" everyone called.

A swirl of colours surrounded her and she was whisked away...

The Letter

Rosa landed in the upstairs corridor of White Lodge. It took her a moment to remember exactly what had been going on in real life, but as she looked around her, it all came flooding back. Of course! She was at the Royal Ballet School auditions, and she was upstairs because Sukie had persuaded her to look at the dorms.

What am I doing?

Rosa remembered how much trouble she'd got into in Enchantia by rushing into things. *I shouldn't be here. I should be downstairs waiting for my interview.*

Quickly Rosa ran back down the stairs. She only just made it. Despite what Sukie had said about having loads of time, as she reached the hallway, the door to the interview room opened and Olivia came out with a teacher.

"Rosa Maitland?" the teacher said.

"Yes," Rosa gasped.

"If you'd like to come in now, please…"

Holding the lingering magic of Enchantia close around her, Rosa ran into the interview room.

Three days later, Rosa hurried home after school. Her mum was in the hall. "Has the letter come yet?" Rosa asked. She half expected her mum to say no, but Mrs Maitland nodded and pointed nervously to the table. Rosa saw a thick envelope with the Royal Ballet School logo at the top.

Her heart flipped in her chest.

"I've been dying to look inside it all day," her mum said. "Open it, Rosa!"

Rosa stared at the envelope. Her mouth was suddenly dry. "I-I can't." She handed the letter to her mum. "You do it."

Mrs Maitland took a deep breath. "OK, if you're sure."

Rosa watched her mum take the letter out, unfold it and quickly skim across the words. She looked up.

"Well?" Rosa whispered – hardly daring to believe – but from the look on her mum's face she was sure she knew the answer.

Her mum smiled in delight. "You got in!"

Rosa squealed and flung her arms around her.

"Oh, Rosa. Well done!" her mum said.

"I'm going to the Royal Ballet School." Rosa

leaped into the air. She could hardly believe
it. "I'm going to the Royal Ballet School!"

Just then the phone rang. *Could it be…*
Rosa grabbed it.

"Rosa!" Olivia gasped on
the other end. "It's me! I got
in!"

"Me as well!" Rosa yelled.

They both shrieked.

When Rosa finally put the
phone down, she pirouetted around the hall.
She felt like she was in the best dream ever.
*I'm going to the Royal Ballet School and one day
soon, maybe
I'll go back to Enchantia again.* She didn't think
she'd ever felt happier. *My real dreams are only
just beginning,* she thought to herself…

Tiptoe over the page to learn

a special dance step...

Darcey's Magical Masterclass

The Spinning Spider Walk

Try this lovely spinning walk and imagine you are the spider from the Wicked Fairy's castle. This movement is called a Pas de Bourrée under and ballet dancers use it to move across the stage. Give yourself lots of space and spin all around your room!

1.
Stretch your right leg out to the side and point your toes, bend your left knee and hold your arms down by your side in a lovely oval shape.

2.
Draw your right leg back behind your left leg, straighten your legs and rise on to your tiptoes.

3.
Step your left foot
out to the side and
rest it on tiptoe, keep
your right foot on
tiptoe and your legs
straight.

4.
Bring your right foot
to your left foot again
and lower into a
demi-plié and then
spin round, before
beginning again.

Magic Ballerina™
Rosa and the Three Wishes

The toymaker's favourite doll and magic orb
have been stolen by King Rat! Can Rosa
rescue them both before it's too late?

**Read on for a sneak preview
of book twelve...**

Nutmeg led the way in through the back of the shop. Rosa gasped. There were amazing toys everywhere! There was a fairy doll dancing on a shelf, a rocking horse who was snorting and nodding his head and a row of teddy bears who looked so real you could almost imagine them hugging you. All over the ceiling were twinkling fairy lights. It was like being in an enchanted cave!

"Leonardo is the best toymaker in Enchantia," Nutmeg explained. "Everyone loves his toys and models. Even grown-ups. He puts a little bit of toy magic into each and every one of them, to make them special."

"Please help," he begged her. "Get my Coppelia back."

Rosa looked uncertainly at Nutmeg.

"Leonardo made a doll called Coppelia…" Nutmeg took a deep breath. "… and she's been stolen by King Rat!"

"King Rat!" Rosa echoed. "Why would he steal her?"

"He wants to get married," explained Nutmeg. "Princess Aurelia refused to marry him a while ago so he's been looking for someone else. He decided Coppelia would be the perfect bride."

"But she's just a doll," said Rosa, confused.

Leonardo sighed. "Yes, but when King Rat stole her, he also stole a crystal orb I had made recently. It has the power to give three wishes to any person who throws it into the air.

He is planning to use it to wish Coppelia alive. He doesn't know how to use the orb at the moment, but I fear it will not take him long to figure it out."

°⊚.*. ☆ ⊚.*. ☆ ⊚.*. ☆ ⊚.*. °

Magic Ballerina

Darcey Bussell

Buy more great Magic Ballerina books direct from HarperCollins
at 10% off recommended retail price.
FREE postage and packing in the UK.

Delphie and the Magic Ballet Shoes	ISBN 978 0 00 728607 2
Delphie and the Magic Spell	ISBN 978 0 00 728608 9
Delphie and the Masked Ball	ISBN 978 0 00 728610 2
Delphie and the Glass Slippers	ISBN 978 0 00 728617 1
Delphie and the Fairy Godmother	ISBN 978 0 00 728611 9
Delphie and the Birthday Show	ISBN 978 0 00 728612 6
Rosa and the Secret Princess	ISBN 978 0 00 730029 7
Rosa and the Golden Bird	ISBN 978 0 00 730030 3
Rosa and the Magic Moonstone	ISBN 978 0 00 730031 0
Rosa and the Special Prize	ISBN 978 0 00 730032 7
Rosa and the Magic Dream	ISBN 978 0 00 730033 4
Rosa and the Three Wishes	ISBN 978 0 00 730034 1

All priced at £3.99

To purchase by Visa/Mastercard/Switch simply call
08707871724 or fax on 08707871725

To pay by cheque, send a copy of this form with a cheque made payable to
'HarperCollins Publishers' to: Mail Order Dept. (Ref: BOB4),
HarperCollins Publishers, Westerhill Road, Bishopbriggs, G64 2QT,
making sure to include your full name, postal address and phone number.

From time to time HarperCollins may wish to use your personal data
to send you details of other HarperCollins publications and offers.
If you wish to receive information on other HarperCollins publications
and offers please tick this box ☐

Do not send cash or currency. Prices correct at time of press.
Prices and availability are subject to change without notice.
Delivery overseas and to Ireland incurs a £2 per book postage and packing charge.